# Pyjama Day!

# Pyjama Day!

by
**Robert Munsch**

illustrated by
**Michael Martchenko**

Scholastic Canada Ltd.
New York Toronto London Auckland Sydney
Mexico City New Delhi Hong Kong Buenos Aires

Scholastic Canada Ltd.
604 King Street West, Toronto, Ontario M5V 1E1, Canada

Scholastic Inc.
557 Broadway, New York, NY 10012, USA

Scholastic Australia Pty Limited
PO Box 579, Gosford, NSW 2250, Australia

Scholastic New Zealand Limited
Private Bag 94407, Botany, Manukau 2163, New Zealand

Scholastic Children's Books
Euston House, 24 Eversholt Street, London NW1 1DB, UK

www.scholastic.ca

The illustrations in this book were painted in watercolour
on Crescent illustration board.
The type is set in 22 point Minion Pro.

Library and Archives Canada Cataloguing in Publication

Munsch, Robert N., 1945-, author
Pyjama day / Robert Munsch ; illustrated by Michael
Martchenko.

ISBN 978-1-4431-3917-5 (pbk.)

I. Martchenko, Michael, illustrator  II. Title.

PS8576.U575P93 2014a      jC813'.54      C2014-902429-0

6 5 4 3 2 1      Printed in Canada  114      14 15 16 17 18

*For Andrew Munsch*
*Guelph, Ontario.*
*— R.M.*

Andrew's old pyjamas were full of holes, so his father took him to get new ones.

They went to a store, and Andrew said, "Yuck! These pyjamas do not feel right."

They went to another store, and Andrew said, "Yuck! These pyjamas do not smell right."

They went to another store, and Andrew said, "Yuck! These pyjamas do not taste right. I'll wear my old ones."

His father took him to one more store. Way in the back was a rack that said PERFECT PYJAMAS.

Andrew looked at the pyjamas and said, "All right! They look OK."

He smelled the pyjamas and said, "All right! They smell OK."

He tasted the pyjamas and said, "All right! They taste OK."

So his father bought the pyjamas.

The next day was Pyjama Day at school. Andrew put one foot into his new pyjamas and yawned once. He put the other foot in and yawned twice. He put one arm in and his eyes closed. He put the other arm in and fell fast asleep.

This was very strange because it was only nine o'clock.

Andrew's teacher put him in the back of the room and said, "He'll wake up in a bit."

Andrew slept until recess, and his teacher started to get worried.

He slept until lunch, and the principal started to get worried.

He slept all afternoon, and even the kids started to get worried.

At the end of the day, the teacher called for a doctor.

The doctor bonked Andrew on the knee, looked in his ears and looked in his eyes. She said that he was fine. But Andrew was still asleep.

Then Andrew's big sister came to walk him home from school. She said, "I'm going to call Mom."

Andrew's mother took one look and said, "I see what's wrong! He's wearing Perfect Pyjamas."

She took Andrew's arm out of the pyjamas and he yawned.

She took his other arm out of the pyjamas and he opened one eye, just for a second.

She took out one foot and he opened both his eyes.

She took out the other foot and Andrew jumped up and said, "Is it recess yet?"

The principal came in and said, "What's going on here?"

"Look!" said Andrew's mother. "It was Perfect Pyjamas that made Andrew sleep. These are Perfect Pyjamas!"

"That's crazy," said the principal. "I say there is no such thing as Perfect Pyjamas, and I am a principal so I know everything twice!"

But just to be sure, the principal decided to try them out.

The principal looked at the pyjamas, and they looked OK. He smelled the pyjamas, and they smelled OK. He tasted the pyjamas, and they tasted OK.

He put one foot in the pyjamas and he yawned.

He put the other foot in the pyjamas and he yawned again.

He put his arms in the pyjamas and he fell fast asleep.

Andrew's mother carried the principal back to his office, and then she took Andrew home.

Then Andrew's mom made him some REAL Perfect Pyjamas. They kept Andrew as warm as toast, even on very cold nights, and they were really perfect because they only made Andrew go to sleep when he wanted to go to sleep.

And the principal?
He is still sleeping.